JY '96

More than a Name

More than a Name

Candice F. Ransom

Macmillan Books for Young Readers • New York

6779086

For Stephanie, who had that famous cake

Copyright © 1995 by Candice F. Ransom

Macmillan Books for Young Readers
An imprint of
Simon & Schuster Children's Publishing Division
Simon & Schuster Macmillan
1230 Avenue of the Americas
New York, NY 10020

Designed by Carolyn Boschi
The text of this book is set in 12 point Candida.
Printed and bound in the United States of America
First edition
1 3 5 7 9 10 8 6 4 2

Library of Congress Cataloging-in-Publication Data
Ransom, Candice F., 1952–
More than a name / by Candice F. Ransom.
p. cm.
Summary: When her mother remarries,
eight-year-old Cammie feels awkward with
her new stepfather and being part
of a new large family.
ISBN 0-02-775795-1
[1. Remarriage—Fiction.   2. Stepfamilies—Fiction.
3. Identity—Fiction.]   I. Title. PZ7.R176Mo 1995
[Fic]—dc20   94-28592

∽ Contents ∾

The Just-Right Wedding

Cammie Bradley was forgotten.

Even worse, she was miserable. The flowers in her hair had wilted. Her fancy pink lace dress was tight across the shoulders. Her new white shoes pinched her little toes and the pins holding the roses to her sash jabbed her middle.

Cammie's mother had married Mike Bixby today. Cammie was her mother's bridesmaid.

The wedding part was scary. She had to walk down the long carpeted aisle alone. The starched crinoline that made her skirt stand out scratched her legs. She walked with measured steps, trying not to look at the people. A woman in a big hat remarked loudly, "Isn't she darling?"

But Cammie didn't feel darling as she stood at

the altar with Mike and the minister—she just felt nervous.

Still, the wedding had been over for a while. The reception was lasting forever.

Music played while people talked and ate and danced. Cammie hooked her finger in the waistband to adjust her scratchy petticoat and gazed out the window.

Outside, a woman walked a spotted dog on a leash. The dog capered around the woman's ankles, wanting to play.

Cammie watched them with envy. More than anything, Cammie wished she had a dog. Dogs weren't allowed in the apartment where she had lived until today. If she had a dog, she'd feed him, give him baths, and play with him every minute.

"Wake up," said a voice in her ear.

She turned to see a freckled face close to hers.

It was William Bixby. He was nine and thought he was a big shot.

"I saw you walk down the aisle," William said. "You looked dorky." Then he burped—loudly.

"I did not," Cammie retorted. "At least I don't burp."

He grinned, unconcerned, and burped again. Cammie knew he was doing it just to be gross. The worst part was that William was her new cousin.

Her new stepfather had a lot of relatives. Cammie had already met some of them at a cookout given by Mike's parents before the wedding. Mike's mother and father were nice. So were Uncle John and Aunt Kate. But their son, William, was just awful.

She wandered over to the table where the wedding presents were displayed. She touched the soft cuddly towels and clinked a fingernail against the rim of a crystal vase.

The days before the wedding had been a lot of fun.

"I want the wedding to be just perfect," her mother had said.

Cammie nodded. "Everything should be just right. Like 'Goldilocks.'" When she was younger, her favorite story was "Goldilocks and the Three Bears." She understood how Goldilocks felt, trying to find a chair and a bowl of porridge that were just right.

Cammie helped her mother decide on the flowers that would be used in the wedding. She even chose the flavor of the wedding cake. Chocolate, she believed, would be just right.

Presents arrived almost every day in the mail.

Cammie's mother let her open most of them. Cammie thought the gifts were very nice, but she wished someone had given them a dog. A puppy would have been the best wedding present of all.

Aunt Kate joined her. "Have you seen William?"

"He's over there," Cammie replied. She didn't add that she had just escaped from him.

"At least he's out of trouble." Kate smiled at her. "Did you meet Rob yet? He's Mike's younger brother. Another uncle." She pointed to a tall blond man. "The woman next to him is his wife, Carolyn, and those are their kids, Jason and Karen."

Cammie's head whirled. Was she supposed to remember all those names?

Kate smiled. "It's a lot to get used to, I know. But we're glad you and your mother are part of our family."

This was news to Cammie. She had no idea she was suddenly part of Mike's family. Why weren't all of Mike's relatives part of *Cammie's* family?

"Time to cut the cake," said Aunt Kate excitedly.

Cammie's mother and Mike sliced the wedding cake. Then they fed it to each other, very messily, Cammie observed.

She was thirsty. At the food table, she poured herself a cup of punch. She was about to take a sip when someone jostled her arm. Punch spilled down the front of her dress.

"Boy, are you sloppy," said a familiar voice. William again!

"My dress!" she cried, furiously dabbing at the stain with a napkin. "Look what you did!"

"It was an accident," William said, but he didn't look sorry.

"My dress is ruined. I have to walk around like this! And I'm the bridesmaid!" She was supposed to look just right today.

"Just say you were trying to water the flowers on your belt," he suggested with a smirk.

Cammie stomped away. Since her dress was ruined, she decided to make herself comfortable. When no one was looking, she ducked behind a potted plant in the entrance and shucked the itchy crinoline. She left the petticoat behind the plant, like a stiff white tent.

Then she stood in line for a piece of cake. She was disappointed to receive a slice without a silver rose.

William stood in line behind her. "This only your first piece of cake?" he asked.

"None of your beeswax," Cammie said, grabbing a plastic fork.

"I'm on my third piece," he announced. "Hey, watch this!"

In front of everyone, William crammed a huge piece of cake in his mouth. Icing clung to his eyebrows and nose. Then he grinned, his teeth full of cake.

Cammie ran to the other side of the room. She didn't want to be seen anywhere near that kid.

After the cake had been served to the guests, Cammie's mother came over and put her arm around her.

"I wish Granny could have been here today," she said wistfully.

"Me, too," Cammie said.

Cammie's grandmother had lived with them when Cammie was little. But then Granny died, and it was just Cammie and her mother. A very small family.

Mrs. Bixby drifted away to talk to other people. Cammie ate a second piece of wedding cake. This time she made sure she got a slice with a silver rose on it.

A burst of laughter made her look back at the entrance.

"Hey, dork face! Lose something?" William pranced around her with her crinoline on his head, like a silly wedding veil.

He paraded around the hall, singing "Here Comes the Bride" in an off-key voice. Cammie wanted to disappear. Now everyone would know that she had taken off her petticoat!

Mike's parents laughed at William's antics. Uncle John snapped a picture. Cammie couldn't believe everyone thought that kid was funny. William was wrecking her mother's just-right wedding!

When things quieted down again, Mike came over and pulled her onto the dance floor.

"We haven't danced yet," he said.

"I can't dance!" Cammie protested.

"Put your feet on top of mine," Mike told her. She stepped on Mike's shiny black shoes. He carried her around the dance floor in time to the music.

"Did you see William?" she asked him. "He's got my crinoline on his head!"

Mike chuckled. "William is a lot like me when I was his age."

"You were that bad?"

"Worse!"

Cammie stared at him. Mike *seemed* normal. And nobody could ever have been as awful as William.

"I hope I never see him again," she said emphatically.

Mike twirled her dizzyingly. "That'll be hard since he's your cousin now."

Cammie's head spun. She had always wanted cousins but she didn't want William as one. "Does he *have* to be my cousin?"

Mike smiled at her with sympathy. "You'll get used to William. He lives just down the road from us. You'll both be going to the same school next week."

They finished the dance. Mike bowed gallantly, making Cammie laugh. For a moment, she forgot about her obnoxious cousin.

The music played on. Men loosened their ties and women slipped out of their high heels. No one looked just right anymore. Cammie didn't feel so bad for ditching her petticoat.

When the dancing was over, Mike's mother brought Cammie a satin rose filled with birdseed.

"The wedding couple is about to leave," she said. "Throw the seed as they run by." She patted Cammie's arm. "Then you can go home."

Home wasn't the apartment in Arlington anymore. After today, they would live in Mike's house. So much to get used to: a new house, a new school, and a new father.

Cammie felt as tired as Goldilocks. Weddings, even just-right weddings, were exhausting.

The crowd cheered as the wedding couple dashed out the door. Cammie heard something else, the sound of someone being sick.

William was throwing up on the floor near her. Obviously he had eaten too much wedding cake.

Cammie hopped aside in disgust. She would *never* get used to that boy as her cousin.

∞ 2 ∞

Cammie No-Name

Cammie stared at the flossy-haired troll doll sitting on the desk in front of her. Across the aisle sat another troll doll.

The dolls belonged to Michelle Powell and Jennifer Logan. Michelle and Jennifer did everything together, like bringing their trolls to school.

Today Cammie had brought her own troll doll to school. She had plans for it.

"Cammie Bradley, are you with us this morning?" said Ms. Quesenberry. It was Friday, the last day of the first week of school.

Cammie glanced around. While she'd been daydreaming, the other students were busy working. She opened her tablet to a fresh page, wondering what she was supposed to be writing.

She poked Michelle Powell, who sat in front of her.

"What're we doing?" she asked.

Michelle pointed to the board. "Copy that stuff."

Ms. Quesenberry walked by Cammie's desk. "What do we do first to our papers?"

"Oh. We put our name on it." Cammie printed "Cammie B." in the upper-right-hand corner.

She frowned at her paper. She didn't have to use her last initial, the way the two Jessicas and the two Davids and the three Shannons did.

Ms. Quesenberry called the two Jessicas, Jessica S. and Jessica R., and the two Davids, David F. and David W. She called the three Shannons, Shannon J., Shannon M., and Shannon C. but sometimes got mixed up and just pointed to the Shannon she wanted.

There was only one Cammie in Room 11. She wrote her initial after her first name because she didn't know what to do about her last name. Cammie's mother's name used to be Bradley, like Cammie's. Now it was Bixby.

But Cammie was still Cammie Bradley. Having a different last name from everyone else in her family made her feel funny. So she used the initial *B* instead of writing out her last name.

She leafed through her tablet. Since the beginning of school, she had filled ten pages. That was a lot of work. Third grade in her new school was not going to be easy.

Stuck between the pages was her drawing of a cocker spaniel. This was the kind of dog she wanted.

Engrossed in her drawing, she missed the teacher's instruction. Poking Michelle again, Cammie asked, "What did she say?"

Michelle looked annoyed. "She said for us to hand our papers in. How come you never listen?"

"I was busy thinking," Cammie said, hastily copying the sentences.

She couldn't help it. There were so many things to think about. Little things, like why the calendar started with January and whether her stuffed animals talked when Cammie wasn't around. And big things, like whether her father would someday come back from California.

She had never known her real father. He left for California right after Cammie was born. She had only a fuzzy picture of him. Once she asked her mother if her father moved away because he didn't like her.

Her mother had squeezed her in a hug. "Cammie, honey, your father left because he hated being tied down to a family."

Cammie imagined a faceless man bound to her and her mother with a rope. The man struggled to break free. Now Cammie wondered if Mike would hate being tied down.

While Ms. Quesenberry collected the papers, a low hum filled the classroom. When they were between subjects, Ms. Quesenberry let her class talk softly.

An office aide called Ms. Quesenberry to the door. When the teacher stepped outside, the buzz of classroom chatter grew confidently louder. Cammie sat quietly. She didn't have anyone to talk to.

Michelle wasn't going to start a conversation, so Cammie took her troll doll from her cubby. Her troll had silver hair and wore a tiny wedding gown. When Michelle didn't notice, Cammie walked her bride troll on top of her desk.

Michelle half turned, mildly interested. "What kind of a troll doll is that?"

"A bride troll," Cammie replied.

"Cute," Jennifer Logan said. Anything Michelle was interested in, Jennifer was interested in, too.

"My mom gave it to me for being in her wedding. I was her bridesmaid," Cammie finished with deliberate casualness.

Michelle's eyes narrowed with disbelief. "Kids aren't bridesmaids."

Cammie sat up straighter, ready to shatter Michelle's argument. "I was too my mom's bridesmaid! I had a pink dress and flowers in my hair! I'll bring you a picture tomorrow if you don't believe me."

Jennifer stared at her, impressed. "Were you scared?"

"No," Cammie fibbed. "It was fun."

Ms. Quesenberry came back into the room then, making shushing motions.

"Cammie," she said. "Will you come here?"

Cammie's heart lurched. Had she been talking too loud? She didn't want to be a troublemaker the first week in her new school.

But Ms. Quesenberry merely told her that the secretary in the office wanted to see her. She gave Cammie the wooden hall pass shaped like a big key.

The office was near the library. Cammie went inside with that floaty feeling her stomach got whenever she had to report to the office. Mrs. Spencer hung up the phone and came over with a brown envelope.

"Cammie," she said. "These are papers for your parents' signature. Please take them home and bring them back tomorrow."

The envelope had "Mrs. Bradley" written across the top.

"Mrs. Spencer, that's not right," Cammie told the secretary. "My mother's name is Mrs. Bixby."

"Oh, I'm sorry. I'll fix it right now." The phone rang and Mrs. Spencer ran to answer it. With the phone wedged between her chin and shoulder, she scribbled over "Mrs. Bradley." Still talking, she opened the envelope, crossed out some words, and wrote something.

Hanging up again, she brought the envelope over to Cammie, with the papers inside sticking out. The name on the outside was right, "Mrs. Bixby," but the name on the papers was wrong. Mrs. Spencer had changed Cammie's name to "Camilla Bixby."

"My name isn't Bixby," Cammie explained. "It's Bradley."

Mrs. Spencer took the envelope back a second time. "I don't know what's wrong with me today." She scratched out her correction and rewrote

"Camilla Bradley" in small letters in the margin.

Cammie took the envelope and left the office. She wished she didn't have any name at all.

Months ago, when her mother began making wedding plans, she informed Cammie that she would no longer be Louise Bradley. Her name would change.

"Will my name change, too?" Cammie had asked.

"No," her mother had said. "Your name will stay the same. When a woman marries a man, she can take his name, if she wants. I would like to have Mike's last name, so my name will change the day we are married."

"But mine won't?" Cammie was still confused.

"Not automatically. Mike would have to adopt you. Then your name would be the same as his."

"I thought only babies got adopted," Cammie said, thinking of a classmate who told how she'd been specially picked as a tiny baby. Cammie did not realize regular kids could be adopted, too.

They didn't talk anymore about names or adoption that day. The busy wedding time came, and then the move into Mike's house.

While Cammie was remembering the discussion with her mother, she forgot to turn by the library.

She had wandered down another hall instead. This part of the school was unfamiliar to her.

She was lost. How could she get back to Room 11?

Someone hissed from a nearby classroom. Cammie saw older kids writing. William Bixby made a face at her. Cammie turned away. It was bad enough she had to ride the same bus with him.

Just then Jennifer Logan hurried toward her. "The teacher sent me to find you."

"I got lost," Cammie admitted sheepishly.

At the door of Room 11, Jennifer shrugged. "No big deal. I get lost lots of times."

"You're new, too?" Cammie asked.

"Yeah. We moved here from Texas this summer."

Cammie felt better. Maybe she would be friends with Jennifer. As she returned to her seat, she noticed Ms. Quesenberry had written "Bennett's 60th Birthday" in big letters on the board.

Cammie had seen several banners around the school with the same slogan. This year Bennett Elementary was sixty years old.

"What's going on?" Cammie asked Michelle.

"Just birthday stuff," Michelle replied in a tone that assumed Cammie knew about the celebration.

On the first day of school, Cammie had learned about the yearlong activities planned, such as speakers who once attended the school and special assemblies. Everyone talked about the school's birthday. Cammie felt as if she'd walked in on a party that she hadn't been invited to.

"We're having an essay contest," Ms. Quesenberry said to the class. "The theme of the essay is what Bennett Elementary means to you. There'll be prizes within each grade. Does anyone have any questions?"

Jennifer Logan raised her hand. "What's an essay?"

Cammie was glad she asked. She didn't know what an essay was either.

Ms. Quesenberry explained that an essay was a short paper with paragraphs and a title, about a given subject.

"I'm sure all of you can write a few paragraphs about what your school means to you. I would be very proud if one of my students won the third-grade prize."

Cammie wasn't interested in writing an essay about a school she barely knew, even if it was sixty years old. Right now she was more interested in finding someone to sit with at lunch.

In the cafeteria, she found an empty chair at Michelle and Jennifer's table. Cammie sat down and opened her lunch box. Her mother gave her good things, like carrot sticks. But she also included fun things, like olives or fortune cookies.

Today her mother had packed one of Cammie's favorite treats: a cracker sandwich, along with an orange, a plastic container of pasta salad, and oatmeal cookies.

Michelle watched Cammie unwrap her sandwich. "What's *that*?"

"A cracker sandwich." Cammie lifted the top slice of bread so they could see the soda crackers lined up on the bottom slice. "It's good. Tastes like lettuce."

"If it tastes like lettuce," Jennifer giggled, "why not put lettuce on it in the first place?"

"Because I like things that taste like something else," Cammie replied. She looked at the limp, greasy nachos on Michelle's tray and wrinkled her nose. "The cafeteria food here isn't any better than at my other school."

"What school did you used to go to?" asked Jennifer.

"Canterbury Woods. It's not like this school at all. Sometimes I miss it." Cammie nearly added that she missed her old home and her old friends, too.

"Cammie's mother just got married," Michelle said to Jennifer, even though Jennifer already knew. "Cammie was her bridesmaid."

Michelle picked cheese off a nacho chip. "My mom got married again, too. My stepfather adopted me and my brother so now he's our father. Did your stepfather adopt you?"

Cammie stopped, the milk carton halfway to her mouth. "I think he's going to," she said uncertainly. "I mean, he might have already, and he forgot to tell me."

"You'd *know*," Michelle said with authority. "You have to go to a building and talk to a judge. It's a big deal."

Cammie put down her sandwich.

"Did you get a different last name?" Cammie asked. If Mike adopted her, she would have the same last name as everyone else in her house. That would be great, she decided. No more mix-ups.

Michelle nodded. "I have a paper with my new name on it. My father said he wanted to make us a real family."

Cammie wondered then if Mike would want to adopt *her*. He had married Cammie's mother, but maybe he didn't really want a daughter, too. It all reminded Cammie of buying a candy bar. You don't really need the wrapper, but it comes with the candy anyway.

❧ 3 ❧

Trillium

When the last bell of the day rang, Cammie grabbed her knapsack and ran outside. She still wasn't used to riding a school bus. In Arlington, Cammie had walked to and from school.

The buses reminded Cammie of yellow dragons, belching diesel fumes and impatient to be off. She hurried between the double line of buses, trying to find number 271.

"Over here, dork face!" William Bixby hung out the narrow bus window.

Even though William lived down the road from Cammie, she had hoped she would hardly see Mike's nephew. But William attended Bennett Elementary, too, as a fourth grader. They both rode bus 271, which meant that Cammie had to see him at least twice a day.

Angrily she boarded the bus. She hated being called dork face. Still not used to the steep steps, she tripped on the top one.

"Oops. Careful." The bus driver reached out to break her fall. "You okay?"

"I think so." Cammie limped down the aisle. Her knee hurt.

"I saw that," William said as she passed his seat. "Maybe you should go back to the nurse. Get your dorky little knee looked at."

"I do not have dorky knees," she retorted.

The only empty seat was behind William's. She sat down, praying he would leave her alone. But he twisted around to talk to her. "I saw you today outside my room. Were you lost?"

"No," Cammie said. "I just took a wrong turn, that's all."

"Oh." The single word dripped with disbelief. Then he asked, grinning, "Did you keep your petticoat on today?"

"I'm wearing shorts, as you can see."

She stared hard out the window. William seemed to know the worst things about her. That she got lost in the winding halls. That she tripped getting on the bus. Most embarrassing of all, that she had taken off her crinoline at her mother's wedding.

For the rest of the ride, he didn't bother her. Cammie was glad.

When the bus slowed at her driveway, William announced like a conductor, "Your stop, dork face!"

Cammie couldn't wait to get away from her cousin.

Like her new school, her new house wasn't really new. The house was big and old, surrounded by oak trees. It was Mike's house.

Cammie opened the side door and walked into the kitchen.

Her mother was sitting at the table, putting wedding pictures in a photo album. By her elbow were several colored paper strips.

"Hi, sweetie," she greeted. "How was your day?" Mrs. Bixby was a nurse in a high school. She left for work as soon as Cammie caught her morning bus. In the afternoon, she was home before Cammie.

"It was okay." Cammie didn't mention getting lost or tripping on the bus. From her knapsack, she pulled the envelope the school secretary had given her. "You have to sign these."

Her mother opened the envelope. "More forms. You would think you had transferred from another galaxy instead of another school system."

"The secretary got your name wrong," Cammie said, pouring herself a bowl of Frosty Puffs. Cereal was her favorite after-school snack.

"Yes, I see where she scribbled it out." Her mother filled in some lines, then signed her new last name carefully, as if she had to think about it.

"Our names are different," Cammie said.

"Yes, they are," her mother murmured absently.

Cammie sighed. She had hoped her mother would say, "I guess we'll just have to make all our names the same now that we're a family." But she didn't. Her mother just stuffed the forms back in the envelope, then resumed putting photos in the album.

Cammie finished her cereal and poured a second bowl quietly so her mother wouldn't notice she was spoiling her appetite for supper. She didn't like Frosty Puffs that much, but there was a free plastic dog in each box and she was trying to get a cocker spaniel. So far she had collected a collie and a boxer.

"What are these?" Cammie asked as she picked up one of the colored strips of paper lying on the table.

"Paint chips," her mother answered. "I thought we'd paint your room. Mike can take off one Saturday this month. Do you want him to take off for your birthday or to paint your room?"

Cammie considered. Mike had two jobs. During the week, he worked at Hechinger's, the World's Largest Hardware Store. On Saturdays, he worked in a store that sold computers. Cammie figured Mike probably wouldn't want to spend his one free Saturday at a kids' birthday party.

"Paint my room," she told her mother.

Her mother nodded. "We can paint your room next weekend."

Cammie's bedroom had gray walls, dark green drapes that hid the sunlight, and a brown rug. She didn't like the room very much. It wasn't anything like her room in their old apartment.

"Can I pick out the color?" she asked.

"Certainly. That's why I brought home these paint chips. Your room can be any color you like. Except black!"

Cammie studied the colored strips. She had never realized there were so many shades of blue, so many different pinks. The blocks of pure color filled her with pleasure.

At last she pushed a strip across the table to her mother. She pointed to a pinkish lavender block with a word she couldn't read printed underneath. "That one."

"Trillium," her mother read.

"Is that a color?"

"It's a flower. This color is named after the flower."

Trillium. She was going to paint her room trillium. Putting the paint chip in her pocket for safekeeping, she repeated the new word to herself, making it hers.

The family discussed painting Cammie's room at supper.

"Trillium!" Mike echoed when Cammie's mother told him of Cammie's choice. "What kind of a color is that?"

Cammie pulled the paint strip from her pocket and showed it to her stepfather. He held the fragile strip in big hands that reminded Cammie of bear paws.

"Hmm," he remarked. "Looks like plain old pink to me. But if that's what you want, that's what you'll have. I'll have the paint mixed tomorrow at the store. I hope the guys don't tease me too much when I order *trillium!*"

"I think Cammie ought to have a new rug and curtains, too," her mother said. "I can sew curtains on my sewing machine. "

"You don't have time to sew with your job," Mike said.

"It's really no trouble. I can make curtains that are as pretty as the ones you buy."

"Oh, I'm sure of that," Mike said, buttering his third roll. "If you sew like you cook, they'll be the best curtains in town."

Mrs. Bixby smiled at him. They exchanged a look Cammie called the "newlywed" look. For a few seconds, Cammie felt she didn't belong there. But then Mike winked at her, including her in the special moment.

"You haven't told me which kids from school you want to invite to your birthday party," Mrs. Bixby said to Cammie. "Time is getting short. We have to mail the invitations. I wish I hadn't let this go until the last minute, but I've been so busy—"

"I don't know anybody that well yet," Cammie said.

"If you invite them to your party, you'll get to know them," Mike put in.

Cammie stared at her plate. Mike had no idea how hard it was to make new friends. In the old days, when it was just her and her mother, Cammie could tell her mother everything and that would be that. But now her mother discussed everything with Mike. Sometimes Mike made suggestions that Cammie wasn't crazy about.

"Cammie, who are you going to invite?" her mother asked.

"Michelle Powell, I guess. And Jennifer Logan."

"Just two?" Mike asked. "Sounds like a pretty small affair. You're going to ask William, aren't you?"

"Do I have to have a boy at my party, Mom?" Actually, Cammie didn't mind boys, but William was horrible.

Her mother didn't see anything wrong with the idea. "Of course we must ask William."

After supper, when she was alone with her mother, Cammie said, "Why do I have to have William at my party? He's awful. He'll ruin everything."

Her mother stacked the dishes. "William is family."

"He's not our family! He's Mike's family!"

"Mike's family is our family now," her mother said gently.

"Not *my* family," Cammie insisted.

Her mother stopped running water in the sink. "Cammie, I know it's not easy getting used to all these new people. It's hard for me, too. But you have to give them a chance."

"Even William?"

"Even William."

* * *

The next Saturday was Painting Day.

First Mike moved her bed and dresser out into the hall. Cammie carried clothes from her closet and her books and toys to the room her mother shared with Mike across the hall. Her mother divided the paint into three pans, one for each of them.

Cammie painted, too. She slapped a brushful on the wall, watching dreary gray disappear under cheerful trillium.

Mike stood on a ladder, swabbing at the wall near the ceiling. He hummed as he worked. Once he glanced down at Cammie, who was working below him.

"Trillium!" he said as if to himself. "I never heard of such a color. Are you going to get a trillium rug to go with your trillium walls, Cammie? How about trillium pajamas?"

Cammie painted her wall quietly. Was Mike making fun of her? Nobody had told her she was supposed to paint her room blue or white. Her mother had let her choose any color she wanted, and Cammie had picked trillium.

When her mother left the room to rinse brushes, Cammie walked out with her.

"Mom," she said, "how come Mike keeps talking about the color I picked? Doesn't he like it?"

"Oh, honey. He's just teasing you."

"I wish I'd never picked it."

Her mother put her arm around Cammie's shoulders. "Cammie, try to understand. He's not used to little girls and the things they like."

Cammie wasn't used to this big bear of a man either. She was used to her cozy bedroom back in Arlington. She was used to walking to school, and having her mother to herself. And, Granny.

"Mike's not like Granny," Cammie stated.

"No, he's not like Granny," her mother said. "But it's time for us to let new people into our lives."

They worked all day Saturday on Cammie's room. The fresh cool walls made her room seem like a garden.

On Sunday, her mother bought a soft rug that matched the walls and flowered material to make into curtains. But even without the curtains, Cammie's room looked beautiful.

That night Mike knocked at her door. "Can I tuck you in?" he asked Cammie.

She sat up, clutching her old rabbit that had been a present from Granny. "Where's Mom? She tucks me in."

"She's trying to get your curtains finished. Won't I do?" He sat on the edge of Cammie's bed. His weight dented the mattress. "Do you want me to tell you a story?"

When Cammie was little, her favorite story was "Goldilocks and the Three Bears." One day she decided to tell the story to her stuffed animals. In Cammie's version, the three bears were Baby Bear, Momma Bear, and Granny Bear.

Then Granny got sick and died. It was just Cammie and her mother. The story became "Goldilocks and the Two Bears." And that's the way it had stayed, until Mike came into their lives.

Although Cammie's mother had stopped telling bedtime stories some time ago, she still would come in and talk until Cammie was drowsy. But what would she and Mike talk about?

"That's okay," she told Mike. "I'm really too old for stories."

"I forgot." Mike slapped his forehead in mock dismay. "You're almost an old lady of eight. I guess you are too old for stories."

There was an awkward pause. Cammie couldn't think of anything to say.

Mike looked around her room. "Are you settling in school okay?"

"I guess," Cammie replied. "Bennett is old."

"It was old when I went there," Mike said, chuckling.

"You went to my school?" Cammie couldn't imagine Mike ever going to elementary school.

"Me, and my brothers, John and Rob. My dad, too." He smiled. "But not all at the same time. Do you like your room here?"

"Yes," Cammie said. She had plenty of space for her things in this big room. The only thing she didn't have was a dog.

She nearly asked Mike if she could get a dog, but changed her mind. That might seem too pushy. She should wait until she was adopted before she asked for a dog. But nobody had mentioned adoption in a long time.

Mike took her silence for sleepiness. He leaned over and kissed her cheek. "Sleep tight. Don't let the bedbugs bite."

She liked the way he smelled, like grass after it rained.

"Umm—" she began, then stopped.

She still didn't know what to call her stepfather. She had talked about this with her mother before the wedding, but Cammie couldn't decide. Dad wasn't right. She had a dad, sort of. Before Mike married her mother, she had called him Mike. That sounded strange now. She had gotten by the last few weeks not calling him anything. But she couldn't do that forever.

"Umm, what?" he prompted.

"Nothing. 'Night—" she said, leaving a blank space after the word.

It was all such a mess, this name business.

~ 4 ~

Happy Birtday

Cammie invited eight girls and one boy to her birthday party. Six girls accepted her invitation. So did the boy—William.

On the bus the week before her party, William teased her about her age.

"I thought you were eight *already*," he said. "You're just a little baby dork face."

"I am not," Cammie denied hotly. She was self-conscious enough about her late birthday.

The girls in her class quizzed her about the party.

"What are we going to do?" asked Michelle Powell.

"Play games, I guess," Cammie replied. "And eat."

Michelle frowned. "Aren't we going anywhere?

My party was at a movie theater. And Jennifer's was at the pool."

"My party will be in the backyard," Cammie informed them. Then she was afraid her friends would think a backyard party was boring. Maybe they would change their minds and not come.

"I'm going to have a really fancy cake," she said. "Three stories high. With flowers and birds on it."

"Well, okay," Michelle said, as if the fancy cake made up for everything else.

The morning of her birthday was bright and sunny. Cammie threw back the covers and ran out to the kitchen. Her mother was washing her big mixing bowl. The layers of her birthday cake were cooling on the table. Mike had already left for his Saturday job at the computer store.

"Morning, birthday girl," her mother said.

Cammie sat down across from her cooling cake and looked at the layers with dismay.

"Will my cake have three stories and white birds and silver roses like yours?" she asked hopefully.

Mrs. Bixby laughed. "Cammie, that was a wedding cake! Your cake will look very nice, don't worry."

She *was* worried. Why couldn't her mother have bought a cake from the bakery? Since she was only having a backyard party, she wanted a grand cake, a cake fit for the occasion of turning eight.

Her mother headed for the porch. "Have some breakfast."

Cammie climbed up on the counter and took down a brand-new box of Frosty Puffs. On the front, below the picture of a giant Frosty Puff, was a smaller picture of a plastic dog. "Free Inside. Collect All Ten Breeds!" the box proclaimed.

Cammie was trying. She now had three tiny plastic dogs: a collie, a boxer, and a poodle. The problem was, it took two weeks to eat a box of Frosty Puffs. Her mother wouldn't let her buy a new box until she had finished the box she had opened.

Now she peered into the box with the small hope that the prize would be lying right on top. No such luck. She knew cereal makers too well. Usually they put the prizes at the very bottom, as a reward for eating every single Frosty Puff.

She had a trick for getting the prize out of a full box of cereal. She took her mother's big mixing bowl from the draining rack. It was large enough to hold the contents of the cereal box. She dumped Frosty Puffs into the bowl, watching for her prize. There it was! At the very bottom, just as she figured.

Maybe *this* time she'd get a cocker spaniel. If she

couldn't have a real cocker spaniel, at least she could have a tiny plastic one. She ripped the white plastic bag.

A collie!

Cammie nearly cried with disappointment. She already had a collie! How could this happen on her birthday? Now she'd have to wait *two weeks* before she could try another box.

Unless—she could eat the whole box of cereal *now*!

Fetching the carton from the refrigerator, Cammie poured a glugging river of milk into the mixing bowl. With a soupspoon, she sat down to eat.

The first twenty bites or so were good. Then her jaw began to ache from chewing. Also she was full. But so was the bowl.

Cammie took huge bites to make the cereal disappear faster. With her chin resting on the rim of the bowl, she shoveled in spoonful after spoonful. Milk sloshed over the sides.

"What are you *doing*?" Her mother stood in the doorway.

Cammie's spoon clattered on the table. Milk dribbled down her chin. "Eating breakfast," she replied.

"Breakfast! You could float a battleship in that

bowl!" Her mother picked up the box and shook it. "Empty! The whole box! Cammie, what's gotten into you?"

"I was just trying to get a cocker spaniel," she said weakly. "But instead I got another collie. I thought if I ate this box, you'd buy me a box with a cocker spaniel in it." She felt terrible. Her stomach stuck out and her face was sticky.

"Oh, Cammie." Her mother handed her a wet cloth to wipe her face. "Even if we bought fifty boxes, you might not get a cocker spaniel. Those prizes are put in randomly—a mindless machine drops them in. You could get fifty collies in a row."

This was not what Cammie wanted to hear, especially on her birthday. So far the only good thing about the day was that she wasn't seven anymore.

It would be a while before her guests arrived. She took an extra-long bath to kill time.

"Can I wear my bridesmaid dress?" Cammie asked her mother. The pink dress had been cleaned and hung in her mother's closet in a zippered bag.

"Oh, honey. That dress is much too fussy for a birthday picnic. Your blue dress would look nicer."

Cammie frowned. The blue dress had only a lace collar, while the pink dress was all lace. She wanted to wear something really special. The blue dress was only a little special.

"I want to wear my pink dress," she insisted. Now that she was a year older, maybe her mother would give in.

Her mother did not cave in to Cammie's new authority. "The pink dress is fine for a wedding," she said, "but not for a birthday party."

Cammie put on her blue dress. Her birthday was not going to be a festive affair like her mother's wedding.

It was nearly time for the party to start. Cammie went outside to wait.

Balloons bobbled from a circle of chairs pulled around the patio table. In the center of the table, Mrs. Bixby had placed a basket of late-summer daisies.

Cammie gazed at the expanse of lawn and still-blooming flowers. Mike had cut the grass last night so the yard would be neat for Cammie's birthday picnic.

It was nice having a backyard, she thought suddenly.

When Cammie and her mother lived in the apartment, they didn't have any yard at all, only a concrete stoop to sit on.

Cammie's mother brought out a basket containing several brightly wrapped gifts.

"Are these all from you?" Cammie asked.

"And Mike, of course," her mother replied.

Cammie wondered which present was from Mike. How would he know what she liked? She wanted a lot of things—a dog, pierced ears, and real gold earrings.

A station wagon pulled up the steep driveway. William and his mother got out. When he saw Cammie, William staggered around holding his stomach, pretending to be sick.

Suddenly Cammie felt out of sorts. William *would* be the first to arrive. She was stuck with him until the others came.

He thrust a wrinkled present into Cammie's hands. "Here. Now you're as old as you are ugly."

Aunt Kate made him apologize. Cammie decided that just because she was his cousin didn't mean she had to like William.

He batted a balloon with annoying steadiness. "Let's eat."

"Later, when the others get here." She put his present in the basket. She didn't tell him the other guests were all girls.

"Poor dork face," he said with fake sympathy.

"Can't open your presents yet. What did you ask Uncle Mike for?"

"Nothing." She didn't feel she *could* ask him for anything. She wasn't Mike's regular daughter yet.

He made a face. "Boy, you *are* dumb. You could have asked for all kinds of stuff."

How could she explain that the present she wanted most was to have the same last name as everyone else in her house? But that wasn't the sort of present you could put in a box.

Or was it?

Maybe, she thought, Mike *was* giving her that for her birthday. Maybe Michelle was wrong and you didn't have to go to a building and talk to a judge.

The thought took root and grew in her mind. Cammie convinced herself that one of the presents in the basket—maybe that flat box—had a paper inside. The paper would say she was Cammie Bixby. That present would make her day a grand occasion.

Just then several cars rolled up the driveway.

"Girls!" William snorted with disgust when he saw Michelle Powell, Jennifer Logan, and Jessica Sanders coming across the lawn. "Didn't you ask any guys to this party?"

"Only one. You." Cammie went to greet her guests. More cars pulled up. Everyone was there.

William quickly made Cammie wish she hadn't invited even one boy to her party. He spoiled the scavenger hunt by figuring out the clues in a loud voice. He popped a balloon by Michelle's ear, sprayed Jessica with the garden hose, and threw Jennifer's troll doll in a tree.

"Mom!" Cammie wailed. "William is ruining my party!"

"You probably should have asked another boy," Mrs. Bixby said. "Someone for William to talk to."

"I didn't want to ask *any* boys! Especially him!"

Then a truck rolled up the driveway.

"Uncle Mike's here!" William cried, running to the truck.

Cammie raced him. Mike was *her* stepfather. But William beat her anyway.

Mike climbed out and swung Cammie overhead, making her squeal. "How's the birthday girl?"

Before she could answer, William piped, "Hey, Uncle Mike, I can do fifteen push-ups!"

"You can! I'll challenge you later." Mike ruffled his nephew's hair.

As they walked toward the house, Cammie felt

shy. William seemed more at ease around Mike than she did.

Mrs. Bixby brought out a platter of chicken salad sandwiches.

"I hate icky green things," William complained, picking out celery and placing the slimy bits on Cammie's plate.

Her mother went in the house and came out again with the cake. Nine candles glowed above pink frosting, one for each year and one to grow on. Everyone began singing "Happy Birthday."

Cammie sucked in a huge breath to blow out the candles when William exclaimed, "Look! *Birthday* is spelled wrong!"

Cammie stared at her cake. It said, in wobbly yellow icing, "Happy Birtday, Cammie." *Birt*day! Her cake was ruined.

Her mother laughed. "I guess I was in too much of a hurry."

Cammie's face fell in dismay. She had promised her guests a fancy cake. Instead of a three-storied cake with silver roses, all she had was a plain cake with "Birthday" misspelled.

Mrs. Bixby cut into the cake. "Who wants a big piece?"

Michelle leaned forward eagerly. "Mmm. Chocolate. My favorite. I love homemade chocolate cake."

"Me, too," William said, elbowing her out of the way. "Give me a great big piece, Aunt Louise."

Cammie was amazed. Everyone liked her mother's cake.

It was time for Cammie to open her presents. She thanked Michelle for the cat pin. Then she ripped the wrinkled paper off William's gift. She lifted the lid off a deep box and took out a doll with a bell-shaped knitted dress.

"I didn't buy it," William said ungraciously. "I found it at Grandma's and she said I could give it to you."

"It looks like it covers something," Cammie remarked. The doll's dress came way over its shoes.

Her mother laughed again. "It does! It's meant to cover a roll of toilet paper. I haven't seen one of those in ages."

In a quiet tone William asked, "Do you really like it?"

"Yes," Cammie answered sincerely. "I do." She thought the doll was a neat present, even if it did come from William.

She dived into the rest of her presents, hoping

each box would contain a piece of paper with official writing.

Her friends gave her games, writing paper, and barrettes. From her mother she received books, new winter boots, and a sleeping bag that unzipped to become a bedspread. Inside the mysterious flat box was a shirt.

There was only one box left. The tag said it was from Mike.

Cammie picked it up. The box was too heavy to contain only a sheet of paper. She slit the paper slowly. Mike's face was expectant as she pulled a wooden plaque out of the box. "Cammie" was spelled out in carved letters.

"It's for your door," Mike explained. "Your name is too unusual to be on a ready-made sign, so I made you one."

"It's great." She tried to hide her disappointment.

She didn't get a paper with her new name on it. She was still Cammie B.

The party was over. Cammie said good-bye to her guests.

William was the last to leave. "If you want to come over sometime . . . you can. We can play with my dog, Stinky."

"You have a dog?" Cammie asked enviously. "What kind?"

"Part German shepherd, part golden retriever," he replied. "Well—see you, dork face."

Cammie waved as he left. She realized that William had actually asked her over to his house. Maybe she'd go. Just to see his dog.

Her out of sorts feeling was gone. In its place was a sad feeling, like the way she felt late on Christmas Day when there were no more surprises. This was supposed to have been her special day and now it was all over.

Her mother fingered the toilet paper doll. "I'm sorry about the cake," she said.

Her mother looked so wilted, Cammie felt sorry for her. "It was a great party, Mom," she said, and meant it.

Mike came in, carrying two grocery bags.

"What's that?" Cammie asked.

"An extra birthday present. Take a look."

Cammie did, breaking into a grin. Inside the bags were ten boxes of Frosty Puffs, and a note that said she could open them all at once to get her prize.

"How did you know?" she asked, hugging him.

He ruffled her hair as he had ruffled William's. "Your mom told me. And I just thought you were nuts about Frosty Puffs! Have another bowl!"

"Yuck!" Cammie said.

Instead they all had another piece of "Happy Birtday" cake. Then Cammie opened the cereal boxes with reckless abandon, spilling Frosty Puffs all over the floor.

Inside the seventh box was a plastic cocker spaniel. Cammie examined the tiny dog, her heart filling with lightness like the balloons her mother had tied to her chair. She hadn't received the gift she wanted most. But she did get the present she wanted *second* most.

And that was enough to make her birthday a very special, grand affair.

ᴄᴏ 5 ᴏᴄ
The Awful-Third-Grade-School-Picture Club

Monday morning, Cammie bounced on the bus. She plopped into the first seat, feeling specially privileged to be in the front.

William got on at the next stop. When he saw her, he snickered. "Expecting a flood?"

"What do you mean?" she asked.

"Those pants." He pointed to her ankles. "A little short, aren't they? Did you forget your rowboat?"

"Oh, you!" she retorted inadequately.

But as William walked past her, dressed up in a blue shirt, she remembered what she *had* forgotten. Today was Picture Day.

At school, Cammie walked self-consciously into Room 11, feeling as if she'd come to school in her pajamas. Next to the other girls she looked drab.

Even the boys sported crisp shirts and many had their hair neatly slicked back.

Michelle Powell was spiffy in a hot pink dress with a matching hot pink hair bow. Instead of her usual ponytail, Michelle's hair flowed in soft curls over her shoulders and across Cammie's desk.

"Do you mind?" Cammie said, irritably sweeping Michelle's hair away like eraser crumbs. "I can't write through your hair."

"We're not writing yet," Michelle said. "We're having our pictures taken first." Her glance flickered over Cammie's too-short pants and plain T-shirt. "Uh-oh. Did you forget today was Picture Day?"

"Yes," she said ruefully. "I didn't give Mom my note either." To raise herself in Michelle's critical eyes, she added, "I was *going* to wear my pink lace bridesmaid dress."

Across the aisle, Jennifer said, "The dress you had on at the party was pretty. I had a nice time." Jennifer was wearing a red skirt and matching sweater.

"Me, too," said Michelle. "It was fun."

"I'm glad you guys had fun," Cammie said. She wished she had remembered about Picture Day. Even her blue dress would have been nicer than the outfit she had on.

Ms. Quesenberry came into the room, wearing a green suit. Her cheeks glowed with makeup.

"All right, class. In five minutes we are going down to the auditorium. Remember your manners, please. We want the school photographer to be impressed with the third graders at Bennett. Of course, he'll see that you are a nice-looking class."

The students laughed politely. Being dressed up in school made them act differently. When they lined up at the door, there was no pushing and shoving. Cammie stood behind Jennifer and Lila Enlow.

"I love your skirt," Jennifer said to Lila. She sounded grown-up, as if she were about to pour Lila a cup of tea.

"Thanks. I like your hair. I wish mine was long enough to wear like that." Lila gazed admiringly at Jennifer's French braid tied with a rainbow ribbon.

No one complimented Cammie on her T-shirt or her blue pants. Why hadn't she worn one of her new birthday presents, like the yellow sweater from Aunt Kate or Michelle's cat pin? She felt like a dull sparrow in a roomful of peacocks.

They filed down the hall and into the auditorium, behind the two other third-grade classes. The photographer had set up his equipment on the stage. One by one, students climbed the stage steps and sat on a high stool in front of a gray sheet. The photographer said something to make them smile, then clicked a button on the camera.

With two groups ahead of them, Ms. Quesenberry's class had to wait. After watching several children pose on the high stool in front of the gray sheet, Cammie realized the sheet would be the only thing showing in the picture. The legs of the stool and the lights on the poles would not be seen.

Cammie also noticed how each student's shirt or blouse stood out against the backdrop. No wonder everyone wore bright colors on Picture Day.

In her gray shirt against the gray curtain, Cammie would be invisible. Nothing would show up in the picture except her shaggy bangs. She would look like a ghostly sheepdog.

Ms. Quesenberry came up the aisle, handing out combs sealed in plastic. The girls began to comb their hair. The boys blew cellophane wrappers at them. Their polite, dressed-up behavior hadn't lasted long.

When Cammie received her comb, she whispered to her teacher, "Do I have to have my picture taken today?"

"Don't you want your picture taken?" Ms. Quesenberry asked.

"No. I mean, yes. But not today." Embarrassed, she admitted, "I forgot to tell my mom. I look awful."

Ms. Quesenberry patted Cammie's cheek. "I think you look fine. But maybe a barrette would brighten your outfit. I brought along a couple, just in case." She dug through her purse and pulled out a red hair clip shaped like a Scottie. Cammie recognized the breed from her Frosty Puffs dog collection.

She stood still while Ms. Quesenberry parted her hair on the side and fastened the Scottie barrette. It felt strange having someone besides her mother fix her hair. Once Mike had brushed her hair when Cammie's mother was running late for work. He had swiped clumsily at Cammie's hair with the brush, not even getting out the tangles. But Ms. Quesenberry's hands were deft and sure. She knew how to comb a girl's hair.

She smoothed Cammie's bangs. "There. Now do you think you can have your picture taken?"

"Yes. Thanks." She had never worn her hair parted on the side. She wondered if she looked as grown-up as Jennifer did.

"That barrette is cute," Jennifer remarked. "You know what? I bet my red necklace would match." She had on several colorful bead necklaces. She took off one and slipped it over Cammie's head. "That looks good. You can wear it if you want."

"Thanks a lot." Cammie felt better.

"Your hair looks really nice that way," said Michelle. "You should wear it like that all the time."

"Thanks." In her borrowed barrette and necklace, and with her new sophisticated hairstyle, Cammie no longer felt drab. She wouldn't look like a ghostly sheepdog at all.

The line had moved up. David W., the first student in Ms. Quesenberry's class, climbed the stage steps and sat on the stool. The fourth-grade classes came into the auditorium, jostling one another and talking loudly.

Soon it was Cammie's turn. She walked up the steps and hoisted herself on the high stool. The lights were very bright and hot. The photographer adjusted his camera.

"Just a sec, sweetie pie," he said to her.

Cammie giggled at being called sweetie pie. She straightened her red necklace and pushed back a stray strand of bangs. She wanted her third-grade picture to be really good. Better than last year's, when she had two front teeth missing.

"Okay, sugar." The photographer held his hand out to the side. "Now, we only take one shot. Look at my hand and give me your prettiest smile. On the count of three."

She stared at the photographer's waggling hand and smiled.

"One . . ."

Just then a voice yelled, "Hey, dork face!"

". . . two . . ."

Cammie's eyes swung away from the photographer's hand toward the auditorium. She squinted in the bright lights.

". . . three!"

The camera clicked.

Cammie's picture was taken. She was not smiling, but frowning! Her picture would turn out awful. She slid off the stool, angry enough to cry. There was only one person in the whole school who called her dork face.

Thanks to William Bixby, her third-grade picture was ruined.

When Cammie got home from school, her mother noticed the Scottie barrette in her hair. Cammie had given back Jennifer's necklace, but Ms. Quesenberry had let Cammie keep the barrette.

"Ms. Quesenberry gave it to me," Cammie said. "We had our pictures taken today. Ms. Quesenberry fixed my hair."

"Oh, Cammie. Why didn't you tell me?"

"I forgot."

They discussed school pictures again at supper.

"My third-grade picture was terrible," Cammie's mother confessed. "My ponytail was ratty and I looked like a sick cat."

"I bet mine was worse," Mike said. "My mother made me wear this ridiculous bow tie and I grinned like this." He grimaced, making Cammie laugh and sputter her milk.

"My picture will be awful, too," she said cheerfully. "William called me dork face just as the photographer told me to smile. I think I looked like this." She squinted and turned her mouth upside down.

"Does William tease you at school?" her mother asked.

Cammie nodded. "On the bus, too. He's always embarrassing me. Like today."

Though she didn't really mind that William had messed up her picture—not after learning her mother's and Mike's third-grade pictures were terrible, too. It was sort of like a club, the awful-third-grade-school-picture club. And she belonged.

"Some fourth-grade boys feel it's their job to tease third-grade girls," Mike remarked.

"William is very good at it," Cammie said carefully. Mike might not like it if she complained about his nephew.

Mike poured himself another glass of iced tea. "Well, here's what you should do. Embarrass *him.*"

Cammie stared at him. "Embarrass William?"

"Absolutely! Throw it right back at him," Mike advised. "I bet he'll think twice before he teases you."

"I don't know," Cammie said uncertainly. William could make her life pretty miserable.

Adding sugar to his tea, Mike stirred it vigorously. "There's only one way to change a situation you don't like. Take positive action. Don't wait for the situation to change itself."

Take positive action. Mike's words were definitely something to think about.

She wanted to change her name. But how? Then she had an idea. She would show Mike that she was worthy of being his daughter. And she'd start right away.

After supper Cammie did her homework while Mike did the dishes. Her homework consisted of learning five new spelling words and a writing exercise.

She zipped through the spelling words, but the writing exercise stumped her. She was supposed to write four different first sentences for her contest essay. But she couldn't even come up with one sentence.

She kicked her legs against the rungs of the chair. Then she gazed out the window, hoping the blank page would somehow fill itself with sentences. When she looked at her paper again, the empty lines stared back.

"You're pretty restless over there," Mike remarked, drying a frying pan. "Need to practice your spelling words with me?"

"No," Cammie said. "I'm doing writing now."

"That was my best subject when I was in Bennett," Mike said. "What do you have to write?"

"Sentences," she replied dismally. "Did you get good grades in writing?"

"A's, most of the time," he admitted. "Writing is important for getting along in this world."

"Not if you use a computer." Cammie was stalling. She wished Mike would hurry up and leave the kitchen. She didn't want him to know she was a dummy.

Now he was putting the dishes away. "Computers do make writing easier." He glanced at her. "Are you sure you don't need help, Cammie?"

"No," she said quickly.

She scribbled the first word that came into her head—*the*. Mike couldn't find out that she was terrible in his best subject. If he thought she was dumb, he might not want to adopt her. She printed a whole line of *the*s, as if she had suddenly figured out something to write.

Mike hung up his towel and said, "I'll let you work, then."

Cammie glared at the messy tablet, then shoved it into her knapsack. Maybe Ms. Quesenberry would forget about the writing exercise and Cammie could have another day to work on it.

But the next morning Ms. Quesenberry asked the

class to turn in their homework. Not handing in a paper would really make Cammie stand out, so she passed in the sheet of *the*s.

"We're going to be spending some time each day on our essays," Ms. Quesenberry said.

She had put the topic of the essay contest on the board: "What Does Bennett Elementary Mean to Me?"

Bennett Elementary didn't mean anything to Cammie. She had only been going to Bennett a few weeks.

While they worked, Ms. Quesenberry marked their homework. Cammie glanced nervously at her teacher, wondering what she would do when she reached Cammie's messy paper.

She soon found out. When it was time for recess, Ms. Quesenberry stopped Cammie from leaving the room.

"Cammie," she said, "you were supposed to write four beginning sentences last night. Did you copy the assignment?"

Cammie stared at her essay paper. "Yes," she said in a small voice.

"Then why did you write this?"

She couldn't tell her teacher that she had written an entire line of *the*s to keep her stepfather from finding out she wasn't a good writer. Ms. Quesenberry probably wouldn't understand.

"I couldn't think of anything," she said, "except one word. Didn't you tell us every sentence begins with the first word?"

Ms. Quesenberry smiled. "A great many sentences do begin with *the*. But, Cammie, a bunch of first words do not make a sentence."

"I know."

Ms. Quesenberry handed back the paper. "I want you to do the assignment over. Four *complete* sentences, please."

Cammie put the paper on her desk, then rushed out.

Jennifer and Michelle were waiting for her. "Hurry," Michelle said, "or we'll miss our turn at jump rope."

They didn't ask Cammie why the teacher had called her back. Cammie's sagging spirits rose.

It was funny. She felt good at school sometimes, like now, and like yesterday when Ms. Quesenberry had given her the Scottie barrette and Jennifer had loaned Cammie her red necklace and Michelle said her hair looked neat.

She felt good at home sometimes, like last night

when her mother and Mike talked about their awful third-grade pictures.

But then there were those uncomfortable times when she felt she didn't belong anywhere.

If only she could paste the good times at school and the good times at home on a piece of paper and have one whole good day.

ᥬᥲ 6 ᥬᥲ

Truck-or-Treating

Cammie bent over the water fountain on her way into school. Today her class was going to plan the Halloween party they were having at the end of the week.

Suddenly someone pushed her into the spray. She jerked upward, spewing water.

It was William, wearing a pair of wax lips.

"Hey, dord faze," he said. Then he asked, "What dordy coztume are you going to wear Zaturday night?"

Cammie was going out Halloween night with William. She would probably have an awful time, unless she cured William of his teasing.

She knew what she had to do—embarrass him back. But he was bigger than her, and older. How could she embarrass him?

"I hope you swallow those lips," was all she could think to say.

He spit the wax lips into his hand. "Is that any way to talk to your cousin?"

"You're not my cousin. Except by marriage."

He shut up at last. Cammie thought she had won that round. But when the late bell rang, he rushed forward, cutting her off.

"Bye, dork face!" he sang, pushing by her.

Fuming, Cammie realized she would have to stand up to him, even if he was bigger and older.

In Room 11, everyone was talking about Halloween. Ms. Quesenberry informed the class they could make party decorations instead of working on their contest essays. She passed out construction paper, glue, and markers.

Cammie, Jennifer, and Michelle began making an orange-and-black paper chain together.

"What are you wearing on Halloween?" Jennifer asked Cammie.

"I don't know. Last year I was an M&M."

"A *what*?" Michelle asked.

"My mom sewed two round pillows," explained Cammie. "I was in the middle. The pillows have 'M&M' written on them."

"I'm going to be a mermaid this year," Michelle

announced. "My mom's buying the costume today. It has a long, glittery tail. I'll have to walk with little bitty steps."

Jennifer attached her length of chain to Cammie's. "I'm going as a witch."

"I guess I'll be an M&M again," Cammie said without enthusiasm.

The M&M suit had been fine last year. But now that she was in third grade, she didn't want to go trick-or-treating dressed as a big piece of candy. Maybe her mother would make her another costume. After all, Halloween was four whole days away.

"I'm sorry, Cammie," her mother said when Cammie got home from school. "I couldn't possibly sew you another costume. Won't the M&M suit do one more year?"

"Mom," she said, "Michelle's going as a mermaid. And Jennifer's going to be a witch. The M&M suit is babyish."

"I see your point." Her mother gave her a cookie and a glass of milk. "But I still don't have time to sew this week. I have a training class two nights. Halloween is Saturday."

"Can I buy a new costume?" Cammie asked

hopefully, thinking of getting a mermaid suit like Michelle Powell.

Her mother shook her head. "Those outfits are awfully expensive. You're growing so fast this year. I hate to spend that kind of money on something you'll only wear once."

Cammie nibbled her chocolate chip cookie in sullen silence. Her mother made sense. But she hated the thought of clumping from house to house in red pillows when she could swish around in a glittery green tail. And what would *William* say about her costume?

Mike noticed she was quiet during dinner.

"Come help me put straw on the flower beds," he said. "We'll go right after supper, before it gets dark."

Bundled in two sweaters against the nippy autumn wind, Cammie followed Mike outside to the shed. He brought out a bale of straw and snapped the wire bands.

Grabbing armfuls of scratchy straw, they scattered it on the flower beds. They worked quickly. The sun had already set and twilight was deepening by the minute.

"Now the flower beds are put to bed for the winter," Mike quipped.

Cammie was wandering in the scrubby brush at the edge of the property. "There's an old fence here," she called back.

"I know," Mike said. "That fence has been there since my father was a boy."

"Did he live here, too?"

"No, but he grew up around here," Mike replied. "I bought this place a few years ago. I remember the stories my dad used to tell me, about stuff he did when he was a boy."

Cammie straddled a fallen log. "Like what?"

"Well, he used to come here to pick chinquapins."

"Pick *what*?"

Mike smiled at her puzzled look. "Chinquapins. They're nuts. The Indians ate them a long time ago. My dad said nothing could beat a chinquapin for taste."

"Did they taste better than peanuts?" Cammie wanted to know.

"Better than cashews," Mike said. "Anyway, a blight—a disease—killed all the chinquapin bushes. But my father found one right along that fence. He said it was the last chinquapin bush and he was the only one who knew where it was."

Cammie studied the brambles around her. "Is it still here? Can we pick the nuts?"

Mike shook his head. "That bush died, too. Dad was a little boy when he picked chinquapins. He used to fill his pockets and eat them on the way to school."

Mike was in such a good mood, Cammie decided to ask him if she could buy a mermaid suit for Halloween.

"Buy a costume?" he said. "As kids, we always made our own costumes. I remember one year I went as a gypsy. My aunt had a trunk loaded with old clothes. John and Rob and I raided that trunk every Halloween. Making a costume is a lot more fun than buying one. Be original, Cammie."

She followed Mike back to the house in a daze. He had filled her head with astounding pictures: Mike as a gypsy. Mike's father packing his pockets with nuts that tasted better than cashews. Mike and his brothers dressing up in funny old clothes.

Before they reached the porch, Cammie had a terrific idea. She would make her own costume! She wouldn't have to wear that babyish M&M suit. She knew exactly what she'd be. Everyone would be so surprised. Best of all, Mike would be proud of her.

Cammie began working on her costume the next day after school. She went outside and gathered fallen branches and twigs from the brushy woods along the old fence.

Using her mother's staple gun, she attached twigs all over an old brown sweatshirt. An old stocking hat with more branches and leaves completed her costume.

On Halloween evening, Cammie slipped the shirt on. Some of the branches stuck out while others hung down to cover her jeans. The twig-and-leaf hat jabbed her scalp, but added the perfect touch. She looked exactly like a bush.

Cammie ran out to the living room. Mike was lighting the candle in the jack-o'-lantern. Mrs. Bixby was sipping hot tea. She had a terrible cold. Mike was taking Cammie and William trick-or-treating.

"Ta-daaa!" Cammie pirouetted, leaving a trail of twigs.

"What on earth?" her mother rasped. "Cammie, who are you supposed to be?"

"Not a who—a what!" Cammie exclaimed. "I'm the Last Chinquapin Bush!"

Mike began to laugh.

Mrs. Bixby stared at him. "Obviously you were behind this."

"No, I wasn't!" he admitted. "I mean, I told Cammie the story, but she made this costume on her own. Way to go, Cammie!"

"You'll have to tell me about it when you get home," Mrs. Bixby said to Cammie. "Have a good time."

Mike put on a down vest that made him seem more like a bear than ever. He kissed Cammie's mother. "Don't worry about dinner. Cammie and I will bring something home."

"Yeah! Lots of goodies!" Cammie grabbed her trick-or-treat sack and ran ahead of Mike.

A yellow pumpkin moon rode low in the sky. They climbed into Mike's pickup. Cammie felt important sitting up front beside him as he worked the gearshift.

"Do you like my costume?" she asked.

"I think it's the greatest Halloween costume ever," he said.

Cammie glowed with his praise. Mike was so delighted with her original costume. Her plan to make him see she was a worthy daughter was already working.

They drove down the highway to William's house. "First stop," Mike declared, pulling into the driveway.

Cammie had never gone trick-or-treating in a

truck before. In Arlington, she and her friends knocked on doors in their apartment building. Other kids, she knew, walked to houses in their developments. But here the houses were too far apart. They would have to drive from house to house.

Cammie slid out of the truck, leaving bits of her costume on the seat, and went up to Uncle John's front door. Before she could knock, the door was flung open.

A big golden dog bounded out. He jumped up on Cammie, licking her face.

"Stinky, get down." A creature wearing a black cape and mask stood there. Cammie knew it was William.

The dog wagged his tail. Cammie happily submitted to Stinky's wet welcome.

"William, your dog is so funny," she said, giggling.

"I'm not William," said a deep William-like voice from behind the mask.

Aunt Kate came to the door. "William," she scolded. "Cammie, hold out your sack. What a delightful costume!"

"Thanks," Cammie said as Aunt Kate dropped in several candy bars. "You gave me more than one candy bar."

"We don't see many trick-or-treaters along the highway," Aunt Kate said. "So we can afford to be generous. William, promise me you won't eat too much."

"I won't. Let's go." He swept out the door with his sack. "That's the dumbest outfit I've ever seen."

"You don't even know what I'm supposed to be," Cammie said airily. "And I'm not going to tell you!"

"I already know what you are. A dork tree!" He laughed.

They drove down the highway. Mike turned the pickup down a side road. He stopped at a house lit by three jack-o'-lanterns.

"We know the people along here," he said. "This road isn't as busy as the highway."

William opened the door and ran up on the porch ahead of Cammie. It was hard to run in her costume. Branches kept poking her. She left a trail of leaves and sticks with every step.

The man who opened the door pretended to be frightened. Both Cammie and William were given several packets of candy. At the next house, a shower of treats rained into their sacks.

"I like trick-or-treating by truck," she told William. "Truck-or-treating! That's what it is!"

They drove to five more houses, then turned down the road to Mike's parents' house.

This time Cammie beat William to the front door. She wanted Mike's father to see her first.

"Trick or treat!" she screamed when the door opened.

"Come on in," greeted Mike's father. "What have we here?"

"Guess what I am?" Cammie twirled and dropped more twigs.

Mike's mother came in from the kitchen. "Oh, my," she said when she saw Cammie.

"I can't begin to guess," Mike's father said. "Tell us."

"I'm the Last Chinquapin Bush!"

Mr. Bixby's blue eyes widened. "Well, I'll be darned! And you're the perfect image of my old chinquapin bush, too!"

Put out because no one had remarked on his costume, William said, "Grandpa, it must be fall. See? Cammie is shedding!"

They all went into the kitchen and had doughnuts and apple juice. Mike's father told the story of his chinquapin bush. Then Cammie modeled her costume again. She loved the attention.

Before the evening was over, Cammie was calling Mike's parents Grandpa and Grandma Bixby. If only she knew what to call Mike, another problem would be solved.

It was time to leave. First they dropped off William. Next they drove into town to pick up Chinese food for supper.

On the way home, Cammie held the warm sack of Chinese food between her knees. "Grandpa Bixby really liked my costume," she said, inhaling the fragrant aroma of twice-cooked pork.

"Yeah," Mike agreed. "You won him over, that's for sure."

Cammie sat back, smiling to herself. So far her plan seemed to be working. She would be adopted in no time.

At home, Cammie found her mother in bed, surrounded by a blizzard of tissues.

"We'll bring the food to you," Mike told his wife. In the kitchen, he unpacked the food cartons.

Cammie dug out the metal "sickbed" tray and fixed her mother's plate, adding a folded napkin and knife and fork.

Mike poured hot tea. "Hey, you're pretty good at that."

"I've done it lots of times." Cammie efficiently arranged the items on the tray so she could carry it easily. "When Mom got sick, I always made her a tray so she could eat in bed."

Her mother always made Cammie a tray whenever she was sick, too. That's how they took care of each other.

"I can't wait to get sick and have you take care of me," Mike said. "You make a terrific nurse."

Cammie was pleased. Mike had liked her costume. Now he knew she was a good nurse. Still, her plan to make herself worthy seemed to be moving kind of slow.

She needed to do something *big* to show Mike she was the perfect daughter.

∽ 7 ∾

The Lunch Box Father

The next morning Cammie stumbled getting on the bus. She'd been awake half the night, trying to think of something big to impress Mike.

"Hey, dork face!" William said when he got on.

Cammie was in no mood for his cracks. "Don't call me that."

He took the seat in front of her and turned around. "I see you're still wearing your Halloween mask."

"Leave me alone," she warned.

William waggled his hand as if he'd been burned. "Boy, are you cruel today! Better watch out, cuz, or I'll tell everybody how you took off your underwear at the wedding."

Something snapped in her. Mike's advice echoed

in her ears. *Throw it right back at him.* She was tired of being teased. It was time to fight back.

Cammie leaned forward. "You better watch out, or I'll tell all *your* friends how you wore my crinoline on your head!"

He grinned. "Nobody would believe you."

"Yes, they would. I'll also tell them how you spilled punch on my dress and ate too much cake and then threw up."

His grin vanished. "I couldn't help it I got sick!"

"You could have thrown up in the rest room," Cammie pointed out. "But you threw up on the *floor,* like a baby."

"You wouldn't tell anybody . . . would you?" He didn't sound so sure now.

"Try me." Satisfied, Cammie sat back. She felt much better.

William faced front and didn't say anything more to Cammie. When the bus arrived at school, he actually waited in his seat until she went down the aisle first.

Cammie marched triumphantly off the bus. She had cured William Bixby of teasing third-grade girls once and for all.

*　　*　　*

Before lunch, a guest speaker came to Room 11. Mr. Cobb was there to talk about his school days. He had attended Bennett Elementary ages ago, back in the thirties.

The old man held up a dime. "Ten cents," he said, beginning his speech. "When I was a boy, that's all it cost to go to the movies. Or to buy a loaf of bread."

Mr. Cobb's talk was dull. Cammie stared out the window and thought about her problem.

Mike thought her chinquapin bush costume was neat. And he'd been surprised by her nursing ability. What could she do next?

Now Mr. Cobb was holding up a rusted tin bucket by its wire handle.

"This is what I used to carry my lunch in," he said. "Syrup came in this pail. When we ate all the syrup, my mother fixed me a biscuit or maybe a piece of fried chicken in this bucket and that was my lunch."

Cammie was glad she didn't have to take her lunch in a rusty old bucket. Her bright red plastic lunch box sat on the corner of her desk. She liked it because it had compartments inside for a sandwich and a drink box.

But it was the picture on the lid that made her lunch box special.

The picture showed the cast of "Happy Family," Cammie's favorite TV program. There were nine kids in "Happy Family," all of them adopted from different countries. The TV father, Ted, was the perfect dad. Ted was always taking the kids camping or building them a tree house.

Cammie watched the program faithfully every Tuesday evening. She had a secret. She believed that the man who played Ted was her real father.

In a way it made sense. Her father had moved to California when she was a baby. Now he was a famous TV star. He even looked like her real father. At least she *thought* he did. The only photograph she had of her real father was fuzzy and out of focus.

The class was clapping. Cammie came out of her thoughts with a start. The guest speaker was leaving. She had barely listened to a word he had said.

"You were a good audience, class," Ms. Quesenberry said. "Now let's get ready for lunch."

Cammie scooped up her "Happy Family" lunch box. Across the aisle, Jennifer took a brown lunch bag from her cubby.

"I'm buying lunch today," Michelle said. "I hope it's something good."

Cammie swung her lunch box as they walked down the hall to the cafeteria. "Smells like pizza," she commented.

"Or lasagne," Jennifer put in.

Michelle reached the cafeteria door first. "Yuck," she groaned as a boy carried a tray past them. "It's spaghetti. I don't like school spaghetti." With a sigh, she got into the serving line.

Cammie and Jennifer found a table and sat down.

A few minutes later, Michelle joined them. "This spaghetti stinks," she complained. "My dad makes really good spaghetti."

Cammie looked at Michelle with envy. *My* dad. Michelle didn't have to worry about what to call her new father.

"In fact," Michelle went on, taking a long sip of milk, "my dad is a good cook. We make pancakes together every Sunday. I can eat six." She threw out this fact like a dare.

"I can eat six pancakes," Cammie said, rising to the challenge. "I bet I could eat *ten* pancakes."

Jennifer glanced at Cammie's lunch box. "Do you like that show?" she asked.

"Yeah." Cammie hummed a little of the theme song, "Happy families are all the same. . . ."

"I think it's a dumb program," Michelle remarked.

Cammie was getting tired of Michelle. Michelle was always bragging about her father. But her father wasn't on a lunch box, like Cammie's.

"My father is on that show," she announced.

"What?" Michelle said sharply.

"I said, my father—my real father—plays Ted on that show."

Jennifer's eyes were wide. "Is that true? How come you never told us before?"

"Because it's a lie." Michelle's tone was scornful.

"It is too true!" Cammie insisted. Michelle Powell didn't know everything!

"Your father is a big TV star? Prove it!" Michelle crossed her arms and sat back as if daring Cammie to produce her famous father right this second.

"I don't have to prove it," Cammie said huffily. "I know what I know."

"Well, I don't believe you." Michelle was smirking at Jennifer. "We think that you're lying, Cammie Bradley."

Even Jennifer looked skeptical.

Cammie was close to tears. She slammed the lid of her famous-father lunch box and ran out of the cafeteria.

When she reached Room 11, she went inside and sat at her desk in the empty classroom. She stared at her lunch box. The father on the lid smiled back at her.

In her heart, Cammie knew the man on the lunch box was not her real father. But she had *wanted* him to be her father because he was the perfect dad.

When the class came straggling into the room Michelle took her seat without so much as a glance in Cammie's direction. Jennifer grinned. Cammie wondered what they thought of her now.

She was too upset to pay attention to the math lesson or work on her art project. At last the day was over.

As she packed to go home, Cammie turned her lunch box so no one could see the picture on the lid. The bell rang and Cammie hurried out of the room before Michelle and Jennifer could make fun of her.

On the bus, she took the seat across from William. She expected him to call her dork face, but he didn't even speak to her.

At first Cammie was glad he wasn't bothering her. Then she remembered their fight that morning. He must still be mad. Nobody liked her today, it seemed. She slouched unhappily in her seat.

"What's wrong with you?" William asked. He didn't sound mad.

"Everything." Cammie handed him her lunch box. "I told some kids in my class my real father is on this."

William studied the picture. "You think the guy on 'Happy Family' is your father?"

"I used to." She wished she hadn't told anyone her secret. Now William would really tease her. "Dumb, isn't it?"

William surprised her by saying, "Do you miss him? Your real dad, I mean."

"Not really." How could she miss someone she didn't know?

Taking a marker from his backpack, William drew a mustache and devil horns on the TV father. "There. He's not much of a father, now." Cammie giggled.

William was right.

Her father couldn't be the dad on television. That father was forever doing things with his kids. Cammie's father had never been there when she needed him, like late at night when she'd had a bad dream. He never wrote or called.

Then she thought, maybe her real father never wrote or called because she wasn't good enough to be his daughter. But she would be good enough for Mike. She had to be.

She had to win the third-grade essay contest.

∾ 8 ∾

Turkey Talk

"Your essays are due Monday," Ms. Quesenberry reminded the class.

It was Wednesday afternoon. The next day was Thanksgiving. There would be no school for four days.

"I haven't even started mine," Jennifer said. "How about you, Cammie?"

"Me neither." Cammie shoved her spelling book into her knapsack. She was glad to be friends with Michelle and Jennifer again. No one had said anything about what happened in the cafeteria the other day.

"Mine's going to be about how I learned to read," Michelle said.

Cammie wished she'd thought of that. Teachers

loved stuff about reading. But she had learned to read at her old school, so she couldn't write about it anyway.

The essay assignment would hang over her head during the long holiday weekend.

On the bus, William noticed her long face. "What's with you?" he asked.

He punched her lightly as he sat down. But it was a friendly punch and Cammie didn't mind.

"It's the essay contest," she said. "Have you done yours?"

"Are you kidding?" Of course, William would wait until the last minute. "But I know what I'm going to write about," he added.

"What?"

"One time in second grade the fire alarm went off and everybody thought it was just a drill, but it turned out to be a real fire. We didn't know it until the fire trucks came." He made *rrrrrring* fire engine sounds.

She frowned. "What does that have to do with what Bennett Elementary means to you?"

"Well, it was real exciting. So to me, Bennett is a real exciting place." He grinned. "Sometimes."

"I have too many ideas," Cammie said. "I can't pick one."

Mike had told her a lot of stories. But those weren't *her* stories. Even William's story was about something that had happened to him.

"You'd better think of something," William said. "You've only got till Monday."

The bus slowed for her stop. As she stepped off, he yelled, "See you tomorrow! Save me the biggest drumstick!"

Tomorrow was Thanksgiving. Mike's whole family was coming over. Her mother had invited everyone to their house for a big family dinner. Cammie had never been part of a big family dinner before. But then, she'd never been part of a big family before.

Preparations for the meal began early the next morning. The kitchen looked like it had been struck by a tornado. Cammie's mother was covered with flour and there were ghostly flour footprints on the floor.

"Baking from scratch is so messy," Mrs. Bixby said.

"I offered to pick up pies from the bakery," Mike said. He sat at the table, polishing silver.

"You can't have bakery pies on Thanksgiving!" Cammie's mother disappeared in a flour snowstorm.

Cammie was helping Mike polish the silver.

Suddenly her mother shrieked. "The turkey! You didn't remind me to baste the turkey!" She ran to the oven.

Cammie and Mike exchanged a look. Would any of them survive this dinner?

Cammie and Mike set the table. They used many of the wedding presents, like the pair of crystal salt and pepper shakers shaped like swans.

Mike set up a card table in one corner of the big kitchen.

"The children's table," he said. "There isn't enough room for everyone at the kitchen table, so you kids will eat here."

Cammie looked doubtfully at the rickety table. "Do I have to eat here, too?"

"Of course. You're the Head Kid." He draped a cloth over the table. "It'll be your job to entertain the others."

"How will I do that?" Cammie imagined herself juggling oranges and pulling a rabbit out of a hat.

"Just keep the conversational ball rolling. You know, make small talk. Only since it's Turkey Day, you make Turkey Talk." He ruffled her hair. "When we were growing up, we always sat at the children's table. Believe me, it's a lot more fun than the grown-up table."

As the day wore on, Cammie's mother became more anxious over the turkey roasting in the oven. She clucked and fussed over it like a hen with chicks. Cammie knew her mother would be a wreck by the time they ate dinner that evening. She thought about her mother's problem, and then she had an idea.

On sheets of construction paper, she wrote "Turkey Hot Line," followed by the toll-free phone number she had seen on TV. Her mother could call someone if she got in trouble with the turkey.

She taped the signs all over the house: one on the refrigerator, one on the hall mirror, one over the sofa, and one on the bathroom door, just in case.

The guests started arriving at three-thirty. Cammie was the official greeter. She opened the door and took their coats.

Aunt Kate breezed in with a foil-covered dish. Crisp, woodsy air clung to her coat.

"I brought a sweet potato casserole," she said, glancing at the sign over the sofa with a smile. "Things been a bit hectic?"

"Wild!" Cammie opened the door wider for Uncle John and William.

"Hey, dork face," he said.

"Hey, turnip toes," she said right back. William's teasing didn't bother her anymore. She knew he wouldn't embarrass her on the bus or at school. But family-type teasing was okay.

Soon the house was filled with relatives. Uncle Rob and Aunt Carolyn sat in the living room and talked to Uncle John and Aunt Kate as if they hadn't seen one another in years. Their kids, Jason and Karen, raced through the house.

Cammie's mother made a brief appearance to bring out vegetables and spinach dip. Mike served drinks. Aunt Carolyn passed Cammie on her way to the bathroom. When she saw the turkey hot line sign on the door, she laughed. Cammie didn't know what was so funny. Aunt Carolyn had no idea how worried Cammie's mother was over the turkey.

At last it was time to eat. Mike and her mother led the grown-ups into the kitchen, where tall candles glowed and the crystal shone. Cammie herded the kids to the children's table. They didn't have candles or crystal, but Mike had put a pumpkin in a nest of oak leaves as a centerpiece.

When they were all seated, Grandpa Bixby stood to deliver the blessing. Everyone bowed their heads.

"We thank you for bringing us all together today in this house filled with laughter and love," he intoned. "We welcome two delightful new members into our family, Cammie and Louise. May we keep our health, happiness, and faith in the coming year."

Everyone echoed "Amen" and then began passing bowls and platters.

Mike brought a plate of turkey to the children's table. Aunt Kate checked to make sure they filled their plates. Then they were left alone.

Cammie saw William eyeing the drumstick. "You take it," she said. She felt generous after being mentioned in Grandpa Bixby's blessing.

"What about you?" he said.

"I only want the wing. You have the drumstick." She was enjoying her role as Head Kid.

Then she frowned. The little kids were carrying on instead of eating. "Jason," she said, "stop throwing peas at Karen."

William grinned at her with a mouthful of peas.

"Quit it!" Cammie ordered. "Now, everyone behave. We're supposed to make Turkey Talk."

"What?" Karen asked.

"Small talk—tiny conversation," Cammie replied. "Only about turkeys, because today's Turkey Day."

William gobbled like a turkey.

"That's not Turkey Talk," Cammie said.

"It's all *I've* ever heard them say." The little kids cracked up at William's joke.

Cammie thought she would start off with some turkey riddles. She didn't know any riddles about turkeys, so she converted the few riddles she did know.

"Why did the turkey cross the road?" she asked. "To get to the other side! What's big and purple and conquered the world? Alexander the Turkey!" That last one didn't work too well.

"You have cranberry sauce on your chin," Jason said to her.

Cammie decided they would have plain conversation.

The noise was incredible. The grown-ups were even louder than the kids. A roar of laughter nearly knocked them over. Suddenly Cammie's mother jumped up.

She looked at the sign taped to the refrigerator and burst out laughing. "I never even noticed this! Cammie, how many of these did you put up?"

"Four. One in here, one in the living room, one in the hall, and one on the bathroom door. I didn't want you to ruin the turkey."

Her mother gave her a quick squeeze. "Only you would worry about me. I will never live this down!" She went back to her place, still laughing.

Cammie looked down at her plate, embarrassed. She had only been trying to help.

Just then William jammed his drumstick in his mouth, like a dog carrying a bone. "Help!" he said around the drumstick. "Turkey Hot Line! My drumstick is stuck."

Cammie broke up. "You better watch out," she warned, giggling. "That bone might really get stuck!"

Grandpa Bixby was telling a story about when he was a little boy at Bennett Elementary. The kids stopped talking to listen.

"I hated arithmetic, so I threw my lunch pail out the window and crawled out after it. I hid in the bushes till Miss Mills caught me. She gave me such a licking." He chuckled. "Didn't matter to me. I did it every day!"

Cammie turned to William. "Can you be*lieve* that?"

"If we left the building just because we didn't like a subject—" William sketched a hand across his throat. "Things were a lot more fun in the old days."

Grandpa Bixby's story began a round of Bennett memories from the grown-ups. Uncle John told about the time he pushed a girl off the merry-go-round into a mud puddle and ruined her dress. Cammie had heard about the merry-go-round, an old-timey piece of playground equipment. Uncle Rob told how he fell off the monkey bars and broke his arm. Mike once took a dare to climb up on the roof and ring the bell.

The stories went on until dessert. Cammie proudly helped her mother carry in the pumpkin pies. After dessert, the men watched football, while the women washed dishes. The kids went outside to play.

William organized a game of touch football. Cammie noticed he wasn't rough with the little kids and let them score a lot of points. Soon it was dark and they went back indoors for second helpings of pie.

The grown-ups drowsed over their coffee. The talk by now was very small indeed. At the children's table, Jason and Karen colored quietly. Cammie and William played War at the kitchen table. Cammie won twice.

The darkness outside made the light inside warm and yellow, like melted butter. Cammie felt a contentment she'd never known before. She felt close to these people. Her family.

Fragments of conversation floated in from the living room.

". . . think Cammie will mind staying with us while you go away?" That was Aunt Kate.

". . . be a load off our minds," said Cammie's mother. "We've been worried about what to do with her. We really need to get away. Christmas vacation is the perfect time."

Cammie sat up. William was shuffling the cards again. He obviously hadn't heard.

Cammie couldn't believe her ears. What was this about sending her to Aunt Kate's? She had no idea her mother and Mike were planning a trip.

She didn't need to think about this. Her mother and Mike were going away after Christmas, *without her.* They obviously wanted to get away from her.

Her good feeling disappeared. If her mother and Mike were going away alone, they weren't a real family after all.

⤳ 9 ⤳

The Contest

Cammie lined up her plastic dog figurines on her windowsill. She had quite a collection now. Giving the cocker spaniel the place of honor, she thought about her newest problem.

It was Sunday evening. Thanksgiving holiday was almost over. She still wasn't used to the idea that her mother and Mike were going away. What would happen to her when they left? She didn't want to live at Aunt Kate and Uncle John's.

Cammie glanced around her room. She loved her trillium-colored walls and her new flowered curtains. She loved the view from her double windows. From her bed, she could see trees and clouds. At night, the sky glittered with stars. Her old room in Arlington had only one cramped window that looked out on a parking lot.

She would come back here. She'd live alone, if she had to. But she'd miss visiting Grandpa and Grandma Bixby, and playing with William. She could get a dog—the cocker spaniel she'd always wanted. But a dog wasn't a substitute for a family.

"Supper!" Cammie's mother called.

Cammie went out to the kitchen.

"Have you done your homework?" her mother asked, setting a plate of turkey-and-cranberry sandwiches on the table.

"Not yet." Cammie retrieved a cranberry that had dropped from her sandwich and squished it between her fingers. She hadn't even started her essay, and it was due tomorrow.

"Don't play with your food," her mother said. "Do you have much homework? You shouldn't have left it this late."

"It won't take me long." That wasn't exactly true.

"Need help?" Mike offered.

"No, it's okay," Cammie said quickly. "I can do it myself."

The last few days had been such fun. On Friday they had gone shopping. But the stores were so crowded, they went to the movies instead. Saturday, they raked leaves, and today they went to brunch at Grandpa and Grandma Bixby's. They had been a real family. After Christmas, though, it would all be over.

A stray cranberry rolled across the table and bumped Cammie's plate. Mike had launched it with his fork.

"Mike!" Cammie's mother smacked his wrist. "I told Cammie not to play with her food."

"Just trying to get Miss Bradley's attention." Then he said to Cammie, "You're kind of quiet. In fact, you've been quiet all day. What's up?"

Cammie looked into his big, honest face. He seemed to like her. And she liked him. Why wouldn't he make her his daughter?

"Nothing much," she mumbled.

Her mother stood, clearing dishes. "Well, young lady, you'd better get cracking on that homework before it gets any later."

Cammie carried her own dishes to the sink, then went back into her room. Sitting on the rug, she sharpened two pencils and turned her tablet to a clean page. She hugged her knees, letting her thoughts wander.

She had to win the essay contest for third grade. It was her last chance to make Mike proud of her.

But what would she write about?

If only something really neat had happened to

her, like the story Grandpa Bixby told about sneaking out of school. Or the time Mike had climbed up on the roof to ring the bell. But those weren't Cammie's stories. Those were her family's stories.

She didn't have any stories of her own. Would it be okay, she wondered, to borrow other people's stories?

Suddenly Cammie knew what her paper had to be about. Licking the tip of her pencil, she printed "Cammie B." at the top of the page. Then she began to write.

"WHAT BENNETT ELEMENTARY MEANS TO ME"

I like Bennett Elementary because it's my family's school. And now it is my school.

Back in the olden days my stepfather came here. He climbed on the roof and rang the bell.

His brothers went here, too. Uncle John pushed a girl in the mud. Uncle Rob broke his arm.

Grandpa Bixby didn't like math. So he crawled out the window. He ate nuts going to school. I think that it was hard work back then.

Now we have a cafeteria. We have a PA and computers. We have lots of buses. Lunch costs a dollar and a quarter.

But it's still the same school.

* * *

On Monday morning, Ms. Quesenberry collected the essays. "I see some very interesting papers here," she remarked. "Some definite winners."

"Not mine," Jennifer whispered to Cammie.

"Mine, neither," Cammie said to keep Jennifer company. She crossed her fingers as she spoke. Her paper just *had* to win.

Michelle turned around. "I hope mine wins."

"David Warren says his will win," Cammie told her. "You both can't win."

"Well, maybe mine will win first prize, and David's will win second or third. There are three prizes for each grade."

That was three chances to win, Cammie figured. But she had to win *first*. It was the only prize that mattered.

At home, Cammie and her mother went Christmas shopping after supper. "Our family is bigger now," her mother said. "We have lots of presents to buy."

One evening they all went over to Mike's parents' house.

"I've found the perfect Christmas tree," Grandpa Bixby told Cammie. "A cedar, with the nicest shape. When you're ready, I'll help you cut it."

All the while Cammie worried about the contest. She kept her fingers crossed for luck, even when she ate. She *had* to win.

At last it was Friday morning.

When the bus stopped in front of the school, Cammie bounded off, nearly knocking William over.

"What's your hurry?" he said, catching up to her.

"The contest!" Cammie panted as she barreled through the double doors. Ms. Quesenberry had told them the winners' names would be posted outside the main office Friday morning. Cammie couldn't make her feet go fast enough down the hall.

William was right behind her. "You don't think you're going to win, do you?"

She stopped so fast he bumped into her. "I *have* to win," she said with such determination that William stepped back.

"It's only a stupid essay."

She steamed ahead. "No, it's not!"

A crowd of kids milled around the glass windows of the main office. Cammie couldn't see a thing. She hopped up and down impatiently.

William jostled his way through the mob. "Move!" he ordered a sixth grader. When he had cleared a path, he motioned for Cammie to follow.

A large white poster proclaimed the essay winners by class. There were three winners in each grade. Cammie scanned the list until she found the category for third grade.

She read the names aloud. "Third prize, David Warren. Second prize, Michelle Powell. First prize, Ashby Smith." Her voice faltered on the last name.

She stared at the list so hard her eyes watered, willing her name to appear in the first-place slot instead.

"You didn't make it," William said. "And neither did I."

She bit her lip to keep from crying.

William walked her to Room 11, even though his own classroom was in the other direction.

"I bet the contest was rigged," he told her. "I know my paper was good. Somebody probably bribed the judges."

Cammie knew he was trying to make her feel better. "I really, *really* needed to win."

"But you didn't." This time William wasn't teasing, just stating the truth.

Cammie's class was buzzing with excitement over the contest. Two students in Room 11 had won prizes.

Michelle Powell was puffed up with pride. "I told

you I'd win," she said, fluffing her ponytail.

"You said you'd win *first,*" Cammie said unkindly. "You only won second."

"Second is better than third. Even third is better than nothing," Michelle declared.

Ms. Quesenberry smiled broadly at them. "Class, by now you all know that David W. and Michelle placed in the essay contest. I've just learned that there were additional prizes awarded. Cammie Bradley, your paper earned honorable mention for third grade."

Cammie sat up, thunderstruck. Honorable mention? What was that?

"Cammie's paper was about her family's experiences when they attended Bennett," Ms. Quesenberry added. "Very original. Well done, Cammie."

Jennifer gave Cammie a thumbs-up sign. "Nice going!"

Michelle said over her shoulder, "I'm glad you won, too."

"Michelle, David, Cammie," Ms. Quesenberry said. "Please stand so we can all give you a hand. Congratulations!"

After the applause, Cammie sank back into her seat. She had won *some*thing, but she didn't know what.

"Is honorable mention good?" she asked Michelle.

"Kind of," Michelle said.

It couldn't be very important, or her name would have been on the poster by the office. The essay contest had been her last chance to prove her own worth. And she had lost.

When Ms. Quesenberry passed the contest papers back, Cammie crammed hers into her knapsack without looking at it.

The rest of the day passed in a blur. Cammie didn't even say good-bye to William as she slumped off the bus. She trudged up the driveway, listlessly kicking leaves.

Her mother was baking fruitcakes. Once again, the kitchen looked as if it had been hit by a hurricane. Mike came home early so they ate supper early.

Supper was a hodgepodge of leftovers. Mike had soup and a grilled cheese sandwich. Cammie's mother had a fried egg. She set a plate with a hot dog and peas in front of Cammie.

Cammie looked at her dinner. She wasn't the least bit hungry.

"I should have baked these fruitcakes earlier," Mrs. Bixby said. "They taste better when they age a little."

"I'm sure they'll be fine," Mike said.

"Well, I hope your relatives like fruitcake."

Mike nodded. "Homemade presents are best."

Suddenly Cammie burst into tears. Her mother and Mike stared at her.

"How can you talk about fruitcakes when I *lost*?" she wailed.

"Lost what?" Her mother looked confused.

She was sobbing so hard she could hardly speak. But before she knew it, she had blurted out everything.

She spoke in a jumbled rush. "I don't want to be Cammie Bradley anymore! I want to be Cammie Bixby. But I didn't win. Michelle Powell won second prize and she's *already* been adopted."

Now that the whole story was out, she drew a deep, shuddering breath.

She had never felt so awful in her life.

Poppa Bear

There was a shocked silence as Cammie's mother and Mike stared at each other. Then her mother said softly, "Oh, dear."

Mike gave a low whistle. "Where do we start?"

Cammie watched them through her tears. It was as if her problem was a tangled ball of string and no one could find an end to grasp.

Her mother patted her knees. "Come sit on my lap."

"I'm too big."

"You're never too big for your mother's lap."

That was true. Cammie found she could still tuck her head beneath her mother's chin.

"Oh, Cammie," her mother said. "I didn't know your name bothered you so much."

"But it does," Cammie said. "Other people think my name is Bixby. Or they think your name is Bradley. I want my name to match everybody else's."

Her mother nodded in agreement. "It is confusing, having different names."

Cammie gulped. "It's not just my name. I mean, at first it was. But now I want to be in a family. Like Michelle."

"What's this about Michelle?" her mother asked.

"She told me her stepfather adopted her and her brother. She went to a building and talked to a judge and got a paper that made them a *real* family." Tears threatened to spill again. "I kept waiting for Mike to take me to that building, but he never did."

"Of course I'm going to adopt you," Mike said. He looked big and helpless in his chair, like a heartsick bear.

Her mother's arms tightened around her. "Oh, my baby. I thought you knew. Mike and I planned to fix everything after we came back from our trip."

"I know you're going away," Cammie said. "Without me. I heard you and Aunt Kate talking."

Her mother sighed. "Cammie, Cammie. You've been worrying too much! We've only just decided to take this trip," she explained. "Mike surprised me with airline tickets to Florida. You see, Cammie, we never went on our honeymoon."

A honeymoon. Suddenly Cammie understood. Of course her mother and Mike would want to take their honeymoon alone. But she still felt terrible about not winning the contest.

"I don't understand about the essay," Mike said. "What did the contest have to do with my adopting you?"

"I wanted to make you proud of me," Cammie admitted. "I wanted to show you I'm a good writer, like you were when you were my age."

"Could we read your essay?" Mike asked.

"Okay." Cammie slid off her mother's lap and went into her room. She retrieved the crumpled essay from her knapsack and took it to the kitchen.

Smoothing the paper with his big hands, Mike began reading. When he had finished, he passed the paper to Cammie's mother.

Cammie stood by, nervously gnawing a thumbnail.

"It's a good essay," her mother pronounced. "I can see why you won honorable mention, Cammie."

"It's a *very* good essay," Mike stated. "You're a great writer. I'm proud of you every day. I'd be honored to have you be my real, official daughter."

Cammie wiped her nose. "Really?"

"Really and truly." Then he added, "But are you sure you want *me* to be your real, official father?"

"Adoption is more than getting a paper with a new name on it," her mother said.

"Do you think I'd make a good father?" Mike asked her.

Cammie didn't need to think about this. Fathers did things with their daughters. She remembered the nights he had offered to help her with her homework. She remembered putting the flower bed to bed, and going truck-or-treating on Halloween.

Fathers didn't run off to California without a word. Fathers didn't believe they were tied down. Mike, she knew, would never do that.

"Yes," Cammie said emphatically. She wanted Mike to be her father more than anything in the world.

Then Mike said, "Put your coat on, Cammie. You and I have some father-daughter business to see about."

"What is it?" she asked, fetching her jacket.

"You'll find out." He grinned. "You're not the only one with secrets."

It was cold and dark outside, even though it was not that late. Rush hour traffic still paraded down the highway. They got into the chilly cab of the truck. Mike switched the heater on, humming a mysterious tune. He turned off the highway onto a side road lined with county buildings. Cammie recognized the county dump, where they brought their trash on Saturdays.

They pulled into a parking lot. Lights glowed in the windows of a low-roofed cinder block building.

"Good," Mike said, "It's still open."

"Am I coming in, too?" Cammie climbed out of the truck.

Mike bent to button her jacket. "Of course. There's a nice surprise waiting for you."

Cammie slipped her hand in Mike's as they walked through the doors. The sound of barking nearly knocked her over. Dogs!

"What is this place?" she asked.

"It's the county animal shelter," Mike said. "People bring their unwanted cats and dogs here."

He went up to the counter where a young girl in a white coat was filing folders. "My name is Mike Bixby," he told the girl. "I have a puppy on hold. I've decided to take him early."

Cammie's heart leaped.

"Are we getting a puppy?" she asked excitedly.

"Merry Christmas," Mike replied, smiling. "I planned to pick him up a few days before Christmas, but I think he needs to come home now. I hope you like him."

She was finally getting a dog! Cammie could hardly wait to see him. The dogs were housed in large runs. They barked and hurled themselves at the cage doors when they saw Mike and Cammie.

In Kennel 34, a small black puppy wagged his tail hopefully. He had long, ripply ears and a wavy coat.

"A cocker spaniel!" Cammie squealed.

"I called the shelter weeks ago," Mike said, "and asked them to let me know when they got in a cocker spaniel. I knew that's what you wanted." He laughed. "Now you don't have to eat Frosty Puffs every morning!"

"Thank you! Can I take him out now?"

The attendant let the puppy out. Cammie scooped him up, giggling as he licked her face. "He's so wiggly!" She laughed.

"Here's his leash." The attendant clipped a leash onto the puppy's collar. "And here are his papers for you to sign."

Mike showed Cammie the papers. "See, you

can't just walk in and take an animal. You have to officially adopt them. That's what this paper is for."

She stared curiously at the paper. "What does it say?"

"It says that you are now responsible for this dog's welfare and that you will love him forever and ever." Then he said, "Since this is your dog, why don't you sign the paper?"

Cammie took the pen and solemnly printed her name. Mike signed his own name below her signature, making it legal.

"Okay," the attendant said. "He's all yours! Have fun with your new dog."

At home, Cammie burst into the kitchen, her puppy hard on her heels. "Mom, look! I have a dog!"

Her mother was taking fruitcakes from the oven. "So I see. Look what *your* dog just did on the floor."

"He's just excited," Mike said. "Cammie will have him trained in no time."

"Let's hope he's trained a little by Christmas," her mother said. "He has to go with Cammie to Aunt Kate's when we leave on our trip."

"William can see my dog!" Cammie said happily. "I hope my dog gets along with Stinky."

"You said you didn't like William," Mike pointed out.

"I didn't at first," Cammie said. "But I do now."

"Well, Stinky and your dog will be the same way. They'll adjust to each other."

"They will get along," Cammie said firmly. "They're cousins."

While Cammie cleaned up the puppy's mess, Mike went out on the porch and came back with a dog bed, a dish, and a comb. "Here are his things. Now he's a member of the family."

Cammie's mother said to her, "Why don't you show the new member of the family around? What's his name, by the way?"

Cammie picked up the puppy. "Gosh, I don't know. He was called Sampson at the shelter. But I want to name him myself."

As she took the puppy back to her room, she thought of dog names. At least *her* name problem would soon be solved.

She played with her puppy until bedtime. Then her mother came in.

"Cammie, it's getting late. You have to go to bed."

"Isn't he cute, Mom?" She kissed the puppy's nose. He was so perfect, right down to the tufts of fur on his paws.

"He's adorable, all right. Have you named him yet?"

Cammie shook her head. "I'll think of something." The puppy squirmed away.

"You could call him Wiggles," her mother said, laughing. "Get into your jammies. One of us will be in to tuck you in."

Cammie was in bed with her puppy when Mike knocked on the door. He handed her a sheet of paper. It looked like the paper she had signed at the animal shelter to get her puppy, only it was written in Mike's handwriting.

"What is this?" she asked.

"It's a temporary adoption paper," he replied. "Until we go to the judge and get the real thing."

She read the printing aloud. "I, Mike Bixby, am hereby making Cammie Bixby my daughter. I promise to take care of her, and to love her forever and ever." She put the paper on the blanket and hugged her new father.

"Never forget you belong with us," Mike said.

"I won't." Cammie had never felt so happy. She *was* Mike's daughter, and she didn't need a paper to prove it. She knew he loved her.

He loved her enough to buy her ten boxes of Frosty Puffs to open all at once. He loved her enough to paint her room trillium and make her a sign for her door. He loved her enough to get her the dog she had always wanted.

Most of all, he loved her enough to give her the family she had always needed.

"Your mom says you need to go to sleep," Mike said. "And What's-his-name will sleep in the laundry room, until he gets bigger. Or else he'll keep you up half the night."

"Can he stay a few more minutes? I want to tell him my favorite bedtime story. You stay, too," she added to Mike.

The puppy yawned, making them laugh. "Better keep it short," Mike said.

"The Three Bears," Cammie began. "Once upon a time there were three bears who lived together in a house in the woods. Their names were Baby Bear, Momma Bear, and—" She looked at Mike.

When she was younger, there had only been two bears in her story. But now her family was complete.

"—and Poppa Bear," Cammie said.

She finally knew what to call her new father.

L